KU-477-586

Grace at Christmas

Written by Mary Hoffman

Illustrated by Cornelius van Wright
and Ying-Hwa Hu

F

FRANCES LINCOLN
CHILDREN'S BOOKS

Grace loved Christmas. It was her favourite day
of the year – even better than her birthday.
She loved the tree with all its coloured lights
and fancy baubles, the presents piled up
underneath it, going to church with Ma
and Nana on Christmas morning and then
coming back for a huge dinner.

And she loved acting out the Christmas story too.
When she couldn't get anyone else to join in she was Mary, Joseph, and all the shepherds and angels as well.

Paw-Paw had to be
the animals in the stable,
even though he didn't
like dressing up as much
as Grace did.

Grace specially liked it when Ma and Nana joined in and they could be the Three Wise Men together, carrying presents for the baby.

"This bit is better," said Grace. "Three parts and three of us. We don't really have enough people in our family to act out the whole story..."

As long as Grace could remember it had been just her, Ma and Nana for Christmas.

"Well, Grace," said Ma, one morning late in December. "It looks as if we're going to have some extra people to stay – maybe they'll join in your Christmas play this year."

"What people?" asked Grace. She wasn't sure she was going to like having strangers to stay.

"You remember Rosalie the ballet dancer?" asked Nana. "My old friend's grand-daughter?"

"Is a ballet dancer coming?" asked Grace. That would be wonderful, like having a real Christmas tree fairy in the house.

"No," said Nana. "It's her sister and her niece. They can't get a flight back to Trinidad, so we said that Anita and her little girl can stay with us. Savannah is just your age, Grace."

"It will be fun for you," said Ma.

But Grace wasn't sure it would be fun at all.
For a start, she would have to give up her room
to these visitors.

"We can't say 'no room' at Christmas time,
can we, Grace?" said Ma.

"Christmas is a time for families," said Nana.

Grace thought, but they aren't our family! I wish
we had a stable for them. But she didn't say it.

She grumbled to her friends at school, though.

"I know," said Kester. "I have to let my auntie have my room and sleep on the sofa."

"We have to have both sets of grandparents and it's all a big squash till they go," said Maria.

"You could come and sleep at my house," said Aimee.

"I don't think Ma would let me," said Grace.

"Maybe this Savannah will be nice," said Raj.

But when Savannah and her mother arrived two days before Christmas, Grace didn't think she was going to get on with her. Savannah was very quiet, and she didn't seem interested in any of Grace's books or toys. And she didn't seem very grateful to be given Grace's room either. The only thing she liked was Paw-Paw, who sat on her lap, purring.

"She's not very friendly," Grace whispered to Nana,
as she snuggled into a camp-bed in Nana's room.
"She's like one of those pink
princesses I decided
I didn't want to be."

"I expect she's just shy,
Grace," said Nana.
"Give her time. It's hard
being in a stranger's home."

Grace hadn't thought
of that. She thought Savannah
was the stranger – not her.

Next day, before the visitors got up, Grace phoned her Papa in the Gambia. She was sure he would understand how she felt.

But Papa said, "Your Ma and Nana are doing a kindness for a friend, Grace. You must make your guests welcome."

"I wish it could be you coming to have Christmas with us," said Grace. "You and Jatou and Neneh and Bakary."

"I don't think your ma would like that," said Papa.

Grace knew he was right, but she felt sad that she would never celebrate Christmas with her Ma and Papa together.

But later that day, Grace heard noises coming
from her room. She opened the door quietly
and found Savannah, lying on her bed and crying.

"Whatever is the matter?" said Grace. "Are you ill?"

"No," sobbed Savannah. "But I want to be in my
own room in my own house with my own family.
And I'm sad because this year we won't be having
Christmas with my daddy back on the island."

Grace could understand this. "I'm sorry," she said.
"I shan't have Christmas with my Papa either.
He doesn't live with us any more.
He has another family in Africa.
But we can try to make it a happy
Christmas for us both just the same."

Savannah dried her eyes
and asked Grace to tell her
all about her family.

Grace was surprised to find that she and Savannah
were becoming friends. She got Savannah to
tell her all about her aunt Rosalie.

"Nana took me to see her dance once," Grace said.
"It was the best thing ever."

"I've only seen her dance once," said Savannah.
"She's usually on tour – like now."

"Would you like to play ballet dancers?"
asked Grace. "I've got lots of clothes in my
dressing-up box."

Soon the two girls were twirling round
the bedroom in Nana's old lace curtains.

But imagine their surprise when at supper time the real ballet-dancer turned up! It was Rosalie, just back from her tour, with armfuls of presents for her sister and her niece and lots for Grace's family too!

"It's so good of you to give them a nice family Christmas," she said. "I have to stay in a hotel and I start rehearsals again the day after Christmas."

"Come back and have Christmas Day with us then," said Grace. "Nana always makes lots of food and Savannah and I are going to put on a Christmas play."

"Then I'd love to join you if that's all right with your Ma and Nana," said Rosalie.

Grace was thrilled – they were going to have a real live ballerina with them on Christmas Day!

After church and before dinner, there was a proper Christmas play in Grace's flat. Savannah was Mary and Grace was Joseph. Anita was an angel and Ma and Nana were shepherds. Nana doubled up as the innkeeper saying 'no room!'.

"Your Nana would never say that," Savannah whispered to Grace. "She'd let everyone in."

"It's much more fun with lots of people," said Grace.

Then Anita, Ma and Nana changed costume and became Wise Men, while Grace and Savannah stayed in the 'stable' with Paw-Paw. He kept wanting to get in the manger with the baby doll, because Grace had lined it with straw.

Rosalie was an audience of one – she clapped and cheered them all.

Then she asked if she could dance for them.
"I brought my pointe shoes," she said.
   And there, right in Grace's living room,
wearing clothes from the dressing-up box,
a proper ballerina danced a solo for them all.

"Did you have a good day, Grace?" asked Nana
when all the celebrations were over and Rosalie
had gone.

"It was the best Christmas ever," said Grace.
"Can they all come again next year?"